Just
One
More

This collection first published in 2011 by Gecko Press
PO Box 9335, Marion Square, Wellington 6141, New Zealand
info@geckopress.com

First published as school readers by Shortland Publications: 'The Horrible Thing with Hairy Feet', 1988;
'Faster, Faster' (as 'The Lucky Feather'), 1986; 'Do Not Wake the Baby!' (as 'Don't Wake the Baby'), 1988;
'Silly Old Story', 1988; 'Monster', 1986; 'The Gonna Bird', 1994; 'My Tiger', 1986

First published as school readers by Wendy Pye Group: 'Marvellous Treasure', 1996; 'The Bag of Smiles',
1993; 'The Travelling Bath' (adapted from 'Morning Bath'), 1988

First published as a school reader by Dominie Press: 'The Tiny Woman' (as 'Tiny Little Woman'), 1997

 Gecko Press acknowledges the generous
support of Creative New Zealand.

National Library of New Zealand Cataloguing-in-Publication Data

Cowley, Joy.
Just one more / stories by Joy Cowley ; illustrated by Gavin Bishop.
ISBN 978-1-87746-767-7 (pbk.)—ISBN 978-1-87746-786-8 (hbk.)
1. Children's stories, New Zealand. [1. Short stories. 2. Humorous
stories. 3. Animals—Fiction.] I. Bishop, Gavin, 1946- II. Title.

Designed by Spencer Levine, Wellington, New Zealand
Printed by Everbest, China

For more curiously good books, visit www.geckopress.com

Just One More

stories by
Joy Cowley

illustrated by
Gavin Bishop

GECKO PRESS

With love to Vita Reidy-Cooper
and her parents Lesley and Jane.

Contents

The Horrible Thing
with Hairy Feet

 Over the river there is a farm, and
on that farm there is a paddock of thistles,
and in that paddock of thistles
there is a tin shed,
and in that tin shed
there is a rickety–rackety floor,
and in that rickety–rackety floor
there is a deep, dark hole,
and in that deep, dark hole there lives
a horrible thing with hairy feet!

One day, a girl called Lucia
went over the river to the farm.
She went across the farm
to the paddock of thistles.
She went through the paddock of thistles
to the tin shed.
She went into the tin shed
and over the rickety-rackety floor.
She stopped beside the deep, dark hole.
'Hello!' called Lucia. 'Who lives here?'
Out jumped
the horrible thing with hairy feet!
It cried, 'I do! And I'm going to eat you!'

'Oh no, you won't!' said Lucia and she ran.
She ran across the rickety-rackety floor,
out of the tin shed,
through the paddock of thistles,
across the farm,
over the river,
and she didn't stop running
until she got home.
The horrible thing with hairy feet
lay on its back and laughed and laughed,
because **horrible things with hairy feet**
only eat chocolate chip cookies.

Cowgirl Katie
and Pronto

 Cowgirl Katie's jeans and hat had more holes than they needed. Her belt was broken and she was out of lipstick. 'Now, see here, Pronto,' she told her horse. 'Like it or like it not, we have to ride into town.'

At the mention of town, Pronto shuffled and snorted. Town had no grass. It was full of cars and buses, and barns as high as hills. He gave a loud whinny that meant he liked it not.

'Sorry, Pronto,' said Katie, jumping onto his back.

Pronto had no choice. He had to leave his ranch and his barn full of hay to go to that noisy town.

Clip-clop, clip-clop.

Beep! Beep! Beep!

Pronto didn't like the way the traffic talked to him. Every time a car shouted **beep**, he wanted to run back home, but he had to keep on walking.

Clip-clop, clip-clop.

When they reached the store, Cowgirl Katie jumped down and tied the reins to a post. 'Now, Pronto,' she said. 'You stay put while I go into this department store. Don't run away, you hear?'

Pronto snorted and rolled his eyes at the traffic.

'I'll be really quick,' Katie said.

Pronto waited and waited. Where was Cowgirl Katie? He tossed his head and those reins came right off that old post. He was free! Now he could go in that barn and look for her.

Clip-clop. Clip-clop.

The glass doors opened up by themselves and Pronto found himself amongst men's clothes. He sniffed the air.

'A horse!' cried a man, waving his hands. 'A horse!
A horse!'

Pronto flicked his ears. Of course he was a horse!
What did they expect? A rooster or a sheep?

In a very short time, there were a lot of people waving
their hands and yelling at Pronto. 'SHOO! SHOO!'
They tried to chase him back through the barn doors,
but Pronto wanted to find Katie. He put
his head into a tiny room.

'A horse!' cried a man who was trying
on new pants. 'Get it out of here!'

Pronto galloped
to some stairs that
moved by themselves. Up he
went, clippetty-clop, as a woman yelled,
'Yikes! There's a horse on the escalator!
Somebody do something!'

On the next floor, there were household goods, glass
and china, pots and pans, pillows and drapes and shining
lamps.

With a crowd chasing him, Pronto could not stop.

Clippetty-clop! Down went a shelf of cups and glasses.

Clippetty-clop! Down clattered a heap of pots and pans.

Pillows tumbled. Drapes dropped. The cords of the shining lamps tangled with Pronto's legs.

What a mixed-up mess!

'Whang-a-dang!' cried a loud voice. 'What are you doing to my poor old horse?' And there was Cowgirl Katie with her new hat, new belt, new jeans and new pink lipstick.

The store manager said, 'Miss Katie, we haven't done anything to your horse. It's your horse that's done all the doing.'

'I'll pay for things that have been busted,' Katie said to the manager. 'Things aren't as important as people, and my dear old horse Pronto is like people to me.'

Then Cowboy Katie jumped on Pronto and whispered in his ear, 'Now listen, you wicked horse, like it or like it not, we're riding out of here. Right now!'

Pronto snorted and tossed his head, which meant he liked it just fine.

Faster, Faster!

Billy Castor had been a pirate, but now he had a job driving a bus. He still wore his pirate's clothes.

He had a green jacket and gold earrings and a black hat with a yellow feather in it. The feather was for good luck.

Every morning, Billy Castor put on his hat and sang,

'Day and night, night and day,
  my feather keeps bad luck away.'

As he got on his bus, he sang,

'Never, never, no not ever
will I drive without my feather.'

But one day, a strong wind tugged Billy Castor's feather out of his hat, and it flew away like a yellow arrow.

'Gone!' cried Billy Castor.

'Gone!' cried all the passengers.

Billy Castor sat on the step of his bus and moaned deep moans.

'Time to go,' said the passengers.

'No, no, I cannot go!' Billy Castor replied. 'Without my lucky feather, I will have a dreadful accident.'

'But we'll be late!' said the passengers.

'Better to be late than dead on time,' said Billy Castor.

One of the men said, 'Listen, Mr Castor. Perhaps I can help. In my pet shop there's a yellow parrot. I can't let you pull out a feather, but I can sell you the whole bird.'

'A whole yellow parrot!' laughed Billy Castor. 'Just think! All that luck sitting on my hat!'

'There is one problem,' said the man. 'To get the parrot, you must drive your bus to my pet shop.'

Billy Castor stopped laughing. As he climbed into his seat, he shook from toes to teeth. How could he drive without a good-luck feather?

'Accident!' he groaned as he started the engine.

'Accident!' he moaned all the way down the road.

But he didn't have an accident. He drove very well. He stopped the bus by the pet shop. The man got out and came back with a yellow parrot. Sure enough, the parrot was covered from head to tail with good-luck feathers.

'This bird is used to traffic,' said the man. 'It once belonged to a racing driver. Here you are. Good luck!'

'Thank you, my friend! Thank you!' cried Billy Castor, giving him a gold coin.

The parrot hopped on the bus and looked around with a wicked eye. 'Okay, okay,' it said. 'Let's get this show on the road.'

Billy Castor drove his bus into the morning traffic. He was no longer afraid. The parrot had thousands of feathers and they would all bring good luck.

The bird hopped up and down on his hat. 'Get moving!' it screeched.

'We are moving,' said Billy Castor.

'You could have fooled me!' said the parrot. 'Come on! Put your foot down!'

The bus went faster but not fast enough. The parrot had belonged to a racing driver. It hungered for speed. It thirsted for speed. 'Give it the gas!' the parrot cried.

Billy Castor went as fast as he could. Shops rushed past. The bus rocked from side to side and cars honked in alarm.

'Slow down!' yelled the passengers. 'You'll have an accident!'

'Don't worry,' called Billy Castor. With all those good-luck feathers, he knew he was safe.

The parrot hopped onto his jacket. 'Faster!' it screamed in his ear. It swung on his gold earring. 'Faster, faster, Billy Castor!'

The bus rocked over the hill and down the other side. It went so fast, that the wheels left the road.

'Stop!' yelled the passengers.

Billy Castor could not stop. He had lost control of the bus. It raced down the hill and into the park.

It bounced over a football field. It splashed through a duck pond. Then it stopped in the middle of a flower garden.

The parrot lay on the floor in a tangle of yellow feathers. 'Disaster, Billy Castor!' it screeched.

The passengers got out. 'We'll walk the rest of the way,' they said.

The parrot followed them. 'Call yourself a driver!' it screeched at Billy Castor. 'Look what you've done! I don't need you. I'm off to find a racing driver.'

Billy Castor yelled back, 'Call yourself a good-luck parrot! I don't need you, either. I don't even need one of your feathers. I can drive better on my own!'

He backed the bus away from the garden, promising to come back and fix up the flowers. Then he drove out of the park. His toes did not shake. His teeth did not shiver. He didn't moan or groan.

'A good driver doesn't need good luck,' he said to himself.

Along the road, he stopped for more passengers. As they got on the bus, he sang in a cheerful voice,

'Never, never, no not ever,

will I need another feather.'

Then down the road he went, saying to himself, 'That feather was a lot of nonsense! Nothing but silly superstition!'

But he kept his fingers crossed on the steering wheel, just to make sure.

Do Not Wake the Baby!

 Clom the caveman sat on the floor of the cave in front of a slab of hot rock. On that hot rock sizzled a delicious egg.

'Perfect!' said Clom, licking his lips. 'Pass me the pepper.'

'No, no!' His wife Wurry hid the pepper dish behind her back. 'No pepper.'

'No pepper?' Clom's eyebrows went up into his shaggy hair. 'You know I always have pepper on my egg.'

'And you always sneeze,' replied Wurry.

'So what?' He tried to snatch the pepper dish from her.

She backed away, clutching the pepper. 'The baby is asleep,' she said. 'If you sneeze, you'll wake her.'

'Is that such a big problem?' Clom asked.

'If the baby wakes, she will cry,' Wurry explained.

Clom looked at the sizzling egg and then at his wife. 'I'll sneeze quietly,' he said.

'You never sneeze quietly,' said Wurry. 'When the baby cries, our sabre-toothed tiger will get upset. He'll roar and roar.'

'I'll tell him to be quiet,' said Clom.

'That won't stop him. His roars will start a dinosaur stampede. Stegosaurs. Tyrannosaurus Rex. You name it. They'll start running and the earth will shake like wet jelly. You know what will happen then.'

Clom scratched his head. 'All I want is a little pinch of pepper.'

'There will be a great rock slide. Hundreds of huge stones will fall down the mountain and block our cave door. We will be trapped!'

Clom stared miserably at his egg which was no longer sizzling. 'Are you sure?'

'Absolutely! Just because you insist on having pepper on your egg, we will be done for. Doomed!' At the last word, Wurry threw her arms out wide. Pepper flew from the dish and floated over the hot rock, the egg and Clom's shaggy head.

'AHH-AHH-AHH–!'

Clom went pale. Wurry held her breath.

'AHH-AHH-CHOO-OO-OO!'

The baby woke up.

She laughed and laughed.

The Woggly Hole

Mr Galumpus grew pumpkins as big as small cars. No one in the neighbourhood knew how he did it.

Jack leaned over the fence and called, 'Hey, Mr Galumpus! The kids at school say you fill those pumpkins with air.'

Mr Galumpus smiled and patted one of his giant yellow pumpkins. 'What do you think, Jack?'

'Nah.' Jack climbed over the fence and landed on the edge of the garden. 'They're too heavy to be filled with air.' He picked up Mr Galumpus's shovel, placed his right foot on it and pushed it into the ground. 'I think those kids got the idea from the word. You know, pump – pumpkin?'

'Maybe,' said Mr Galumpus who was weeding around the pumpkin vines. He looked up at Jack. 'Don't dig with that. It's a woggly shovel. It'll get you into trouble.'

Jack dug up a mound of earth. 'It's just a plain old shovel.'

'Not at all,' said Mr Galumpus. 'A woggly shovel makes a woggly hole that will follow you to the end of the earth.'

Jack laughed. Mr Galumpus was always teasing him. Again Jack put his foot on the shovel. While his neighbour weeded the pumpkins, he dug a deep hole.

Minutes later, Jack's mother called over the fence. 'Jack, dear. Wash your hands. It's time for supper.'

As Jack ran across the grass, he heard a squishy noise behind him.

He stopped and turned. There, in his family's lawn, was the hole he had dug in Mr Galumpus's garden. It was like a mouth with grassy lips, and it looked as though it was waiting to say something. Jack got a strange feeling in his stomach. He ran up the path, into the house, and slammed the door. Wow! What kind of hole could follow people? He washed the dirt off his hands and went to the table.

His mother smiled at him. 'Ham salad,' she said. Then she put her head on one side. 'What's making that noise?'

'What noise?' asked Jack.

'That crunchy, rattly noise,' his mother replied. A second later, she screamed, 'Termites! We've got termites!'

Jack swung around and stared at the dining room floor. Directly behind his chair was the hole, fringed with ragged carpet. In it, he saw broken floor boards, the gap under the house and a pit in the dry earth the same depth as the one he had dug at Mr Galumpus's place.

Jack's parents said it was the oddest case of termites they had ever seen. The hole kept shifting. When a new hole appeared the old hole closed over as though it had never existed. What was even more strange, the holes seemed to be following Jack.

Jack tried to tell them this was not termites. This was a woggly hole dug by a woggly shovel, and it would follow him to the end of the earth. But Jack's mother and father preferred the termite explanation. They kissed Jack goodnight, feet astride the hole beside his bed.

'We'll phone the Pest Company first thing in the morning,' Jack's father said.

The next morning, the woggly hole left the house and followed Jack along the road to school. The noise it made was embarrassing: squishes, crunches and rattles, like a giant upset stomach.

'Oh my goodness! That hole!' cried Jack's friend Letitia.

'It's following you like a puppy.'

Jack looked over his shoulder and wished the hole was a puppy. 'Don't put your foot in it,' he warned Letitia.

Miss Sparks did not like the hole in her classroom floor. 'Does that hole belong to you, Jack?' she said in a stern voice.

'Yes, Miss Sparks,' Jack replied.

'Take it out and get rid of it!' Miss Sparks said.

It was time to visit Mr Galumpus and ask for advice.

'I did warn you about that shovel,' Mr Galumpus said.

'I know,' said Jack. 'I'm sorry. Why does the hole follow me?'

'It wants something,' said Mr Galumpus.

'Like what?' said Jack.

'You should know that,' said Mr Galumpus. 'Tell me, why do people dig holes?'

'To plant things,' said Jack.

'Exactly!' said Mr Galumpus and he gave Jack five bean seeds. 'Take the woggly hole home and plant these in it.'

Jack did as he was told. As soon as he dropped the seeds into the woggly hole, it gave a little sigh and closed its squishy mouth. It did not follow Jack into the house, but stayed as quiet as a mouse in the flower garden.

The next morning, when Jack looked out, he saw five big bean trees reaching up to the sky.

But that is the beginning of another story.

Silly Old Story

An alligator jumped into Uncle Tumu's well. It was a rough, tough alligator with snippy-snappy jaws. Uncle Tumu could not get water from his well to cook rice for his supper.

Uncle Tumu said to the dog, 'Good Dog, kind Dog, please bark at the silly old alligator and chase it away from the well. Then I will get water to cook rice for my supper.'

But the dog would not bark.

So Uncle Tumu went to the goat. 'Good Goat, kind Goat, please bleat at the silly old dog who will bark at the silly old alligator and chase it away from the well. I need water to cook rice for my supper.'

But the goat would not bleat.

Uncle Tumu said to the buffalo, 'Good Buffalo, kind Buffalo, please bellow at the silly old goat who will bleat at the silly old dog who will bark at the silly old alligator and chase it away from my well. I want to get some water to cook rice for my supper.'

But the buffalo would not bellow.

Uncle Tumu went to the monkey. 'Good Monkey, kind Monkey, please scream at the silly old buffalo. Then the silly old buffalo will bellow at the silly old goat who will bleat at the silly old dog who will bark at the silly old alligator and chase him away from my well, so I can get water to cook rice for my supper.'

But the monkey would not scream.

Uncle Tumu said to the lion, 'Good Lion, kind Lion, please roar at the silly old monkey. Then the silly old monkey will scream at the silly old buffalo who will bellow at the silly old goat who will bleat at the silly old dog who will bark at the silly old alligator and chase it away from the

well. I want water to cook rice for my supper.'

But the lion would not roar.

At that moment, the wind blew the mango tree. A big mango fell plop on the lion's tail. The lion thought it was being attacked. It jumped with fright and roared a great roar!

The monkey jumped with fright and screamed a great scream.

The buffalo jumped with fright and bellowed a great bellow.

The goat jumped with fright and bleated a great bleat.

The dog jumped with fright and barked a great bark.

The alligator jumped with fright and ran away from the well, snipping and snapping its jaws.

At last, Uncle Tumu could draw water from the well to cook rice for his supper. He cooked enough for himself, enough for the dog, enough for the goat, enough for the buffalo, enough for the monkey, and enough for the lion. There was even enough for the silly old alligator.

What a silly old story!

Clodhoppers

 Farmer Clyde's boots were so old that his toes stuck out the end. It was time for a new pair. He filled the old boots with dirt, planted parsley in them, and left them in the back porch. Then he went to town in his best clothes and shoes, to visit the Farm Supply store.

Now, Farmer Clyde was always in search of a bargain. He walked around the store, looking at leather boots, rubber boots and plastic boots, and he grumbled loudly at the prices.

'Look at this!' He flapped a price tag at the storekeeper. 'Twice the cost of my old boots!'

The shopkeeper sighed. 'When did you buy your old boots?'

'Only ten years ago.'

'Times have changed,' said the storekeeper.

'Changed, all right,' snapped Farmer Clyde. 'This is daylight robbery.'

The storekeeper shrugged. 'Why don't you look in the second-foot shop?'

The farmer frowned. 'Second whatsit?'

'Like second-hand, only it's second-foot,' replied the storekeeper. 'They stock used shoes and boots. They're cheap, but you have to be careful what you buy. Some of that stuff is a bit tricky.'

Farmer Clyde heard nothing after the word 'cheap'. Quick as a blink, he was out in the street and hurrying towards the second-foot store tucked away at the back of a narrow lane.

The shop was dark inside and smelled like sweaty feet, but to anyone looking for a bargain, it was heaven.

Mountains of shoes and boots – all colours, all sizes, slightly shabby but still with a lot of walking in them – were on sale for less than the cost of a cup of coffee a pair.

'I want farm boots,' the farmer said to the woman knitting behind the counter.

She waved her hand at a selection of big boots with fat toes and untidy laces, but as Farmer Clyde reached for the newest pair, she said, 'No, not the clodhoppers. They're too fast for farm work.'

'Fast suits me fine,' he said.

'Are you sure? A pair of clodhoppers takes some managing.'

Farmer Clyde snorted. 'Me manage boots? Come on, lady, I was born in boots. These clodhoppers are exactly my size.' He didn't tell her that they were the best pair of boots he'd seen, for fear she'd increase the price. He grabbed them, his hands trembling with excitement. 'I'll take them.'

Back home, Farmer Clyde took off his shoes and sat on the porch to examine his bargain. The clodhoppers were nearly new, of fine leather with steel toe-caps and rippled soles as thick as the tread on his tractor tyres.

'Cost me less than half a loaf of bread,' he said, as he thrust in one foot, then the other. He pulled up the laces and tied them tight, then he stood up. 'A perfect fit,' he said, stamping his feet on the path.

The stamping seemed to make the boots come alive. With amazing energy, they lifted his feet up, down, up, down, in a quick march along the path, past the clothesline, through the gate and across a field of new spring grass.

'Remarkable!' he cried. 'I can go anywhere I want without the slightest effort.' Farmer Clyde changed direction and let the boots take him over the hill to where his fine herd of black and white cows grazed contentedly in the sun. 'I can walk all day and never get tired.'

As he strode around the herd, he imagined all the extra money he could make with these wonderful clodhoppers. He'd go twice as far, twice as fast, milk twice the number of cows, and double his income. Fantastic!

He turned back for the house, marched up the path and tried to stop at the steps. But the clodhoppers kept on going, over the porch and *wham* into the back door. As Farmer Clyde rubbed his sore nose, the boots rose up and down, kicking at the door until he opened it. Into the house they stamped, through the kitchen and down the hall. He saw the glass panel of the front door coming up fast and managed to reach the catch just in time to keep the boots from splintering it. Out the front door, past the mailbox and onto the road he travelled.

The clodhoppers were going even faster now. Nothing would make them stop except to take them off. Farmer

Clyde bent to untie the laces, but he had knotted them and the knots were impossible to undo while the boots were marching. His legs were being pumped up and down like pistons. Thud. Thud. The clodhoppers were spattered with grass and the thick soles were filled with cowpats. He managed to turn back towards the house, but he was going so fast that the clodhoppers were hard to steer. They took him directly to the pigpen.

The pigs thought the farmer was going to feed them. They squealed joyfully and ran after him, but even their hungry haste could not match the busy boots. Farmer Clyde found himself squelching through mud and heading for the pig pond. He called the pigs and the boots bad names as the thick, stinky mud splashed over his best trousers and jacket, but the clodhoppers kept going. Even though they marched under their own power, his legs were getting very tired. His muscles ached. His knees were sore. He would have to do something soon.

As he raced through the knee-deep pond and out of the pigpen, he had an idea. He threw himself into a patch of long grass and lay on his back, feet in the air. Surely the boots would stop. But no. The clodhoppers kicked the air so that lumps of piggy mud fell on his face. Then the boots rolled him over until they found the grass. They hauled him up and in seconds they were away again. Thud, thud, thud, thud. All he could do was go with them.

With his last bit of fading strength, Farmer Clyde managed to steer the boots towards the barn. As he galloped past the tool bench, he snatched up a sharp chisel. He bent over and slashed at the boot laces until they came apart. The front of the boots fell open and his feet slid about inside. It was easy then to tumble backwards and kick the clodhoppers into the air. He lay on the floor of the barn, panting, while the monstrous boots fell on their sides, gave a little quiver and were still.

That was the end of bargain hunting. The next day, the clodhoppers sat on the back porch, as quiet as you please, filled with dirt and freshly-planted garlic. As for Farmer Clyde, he was in town, visiting the Dry Cleaners and the Farm Supply store.

Monster

 When Monster got sick, she went to the doctor.

'What is your name?' the doctor asked.

'Monster,' she replied.

'Are you normally so green?' he asked.

'No,' she said. 'I go this colour when I am sick. Please help me. I don't feel like going to work.'

'What work do you do?' asked the doctor.

'Mischief.'

'Oh,' said the doctor. 'What sort of mischief?'

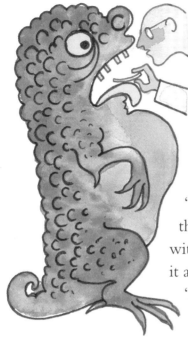

'All sorts,' said Monster.
'I frighten cats and dogs.
I bounce on chairs when my
feet are dirty. I pop party
balloons and pick the icing
off birthday cakes. I squeeze
toothpaste out of tubes. I
make blah-blah faces at the
post-lady.'

'No wonder you are sick,' said
the doctor. 'You are worn out
with mischief. You'll have to stop
it at once.'

'But I've done mischief all my
life,' said Monster. 'I can't give it
up now.'

'You'll have to try,' said the doctor. 'Look at you! You're
greener than a frog!'

So Monster went home and tried to give up mischief.
It was very hard. But when she stopped scaring dogs and
cats, she felt better. The cats and dogs even began to like her.

She washed her feet more often, and stopped bouncing on chairs. Her dark green colour began to fade.

At the next party, she did not pop the children's balloons. Nor did she pick the icing off the birthday cake. The children enjoyed the party and so did she.

'Your skin is a lovely gold,' one of the children said.

When Monster brushed her teeth, she noticed that the green colour had completely disappeared. 'I'm better!' she said as she carefully put the cap back on the toothpaste. 'The doctor was right! Mischief is bad for me! There will be no more mischief from now on!'

But every now and then, Monster would forget and make blah–blah faces at the post-lady.

The Gonna Bird

The old man and the old woman found a stray Gonna bird in the park. It was a very beautiful bird, with long pink feathers, a purple beak and golden eyes that looked half asleep.

'Please take me home with you,' the Gonna bird pleaded.

So the old man and the old woman took the Gonna bird home and made a nest of silk cushions for it in their living room. What they didn't know was that Gonna birds are extremely lazy. Once they have found someone to look after them, they don't stir a feather. So all day, that bird lay on its cushions, and squawked for attention.

'Bring me my breakfast! I want some peeled grapes! Brush my feathers! Plump up my cushions!'

It wasn't enough that the old couple had to peel the grapes. They also had to pop them into the wide-open purple beak.

'Gonna bird,' said the woman, 'you are certainly a lot of work.'

After two weeks, the old man and the old woman were tired of working all day for the lazy bird.

'Gonna bird, when are you going to get off those cushions and get some exercise?' the man asked.

'I'm gonna do it soon,' replied the bird.

'When are you going to eat your breakfast like other birds?' demanded the woman.

'I'm gonna do it tomorrow,' said the bird but, of course, it didn't.

The man and woman tried to be gentle and encouraging. The man sat at the piano and the woman sang, 'Tra-la-la! Too-loo-loo-loo.' Then they said to the

bird, 'Come on, Gonna bird, sing with us! You can do it!'

The bird closed its eyes.

'All birds can sing,' said the woman. 'Just try. Tra-la-la! Too-loo-loo-loo!'

'Stop that noise,' said the bird. 'I can't get to sleep.'

So the old man and the old woman tried something else. 'It's a lovely day, Gonna bird. Come for a walk in the park.'

'Only if you carry me,' the bird replied.

The man and woman took turns to carry the heavy bird around the park. 'When will you walk by yourself?' the man grumbled.

'I'm gonna do it tomorrow,' said the bird.

'Your tomorrows never come,' said the woman.

The bird laughed. 'Of course tomorrow never comes. If it did, it would be today,' and it cackled as though this was very funny.

The next day, the old man and the old woman sat down at the table to eat their breakfast.

'Get me *my* breakfast!' screeched the Gonna bird.

'Tomorrow,' said the old man.

'No!' cried the bird. 'Now!'

'We can't,' said the old woman, putting down her spoon. 'Now we are going for a walk in the park.'

The bird ruffled its feathers. 'Take me! Take me!'

'We'll take you tomorrow,' said the woman.

The Gonna bird sat by itself in the empty house. There was no one to talk to it, no one to feed it, no one to brush its fine feathers. It felt lonely and very hungry.

When the man and woman came back from their walk, the bird met them at the door. 'Tra-la-la! Too-loo-loo-loo!' it sang.

The man and the woman looked at each other and smiled. Then the woman put food in the bird's dish and said, 'Bird, when are you going to feed yourself?'

'I'm gonna do it right now!' said the bird.

And that's exactly what it did.

Halifax Tickle

 Halifax Tickle was a garden elf with big flat feet and eyes like green plums. Most garden elves, being very shy, hid in large gardens full of trees and wild weeds. But Halifax Tickle liked small gardens full of good things to eat. Whenever he was discovered, he would take his willow-wood hoe and his pet snail, Slimy, and wander off to look for a new home. That is how he discovered Greenmeadow School.

Late spring, when the days were warm and the rain soft, the junior class planted a garden of beans, curly peas, corn

and tomatoes. Mrs Poutu, the class teacher, showed
the children how to care for the garden and by
midsummer the vegetables were almost ready to eat.

Each day the children took turns working between the
green rows.

'Jordan,' said Mrs Poutu. 'Today you can pull out weeds.
Mike, you do the watering.'

On her hands and knees, Jordan moved along the dark
earth between the corn and the
peas. She pulled a weed here
and a weed there.

When she saw a big, green,
hairy plant, she grabbed it
with both hands.

'Ouch!' something
squeaked. 'That's my big toe!'

Jordan fell backwards.
The corn stalks parted and
out came a small, angry
garden elf, eyes rolling like
green golf balls.

'Oops,' said Jordan. 'Sorry. I thought you were a weed.'

Halifax Tickle rubbed his toe. 'Don't you know the difference between a weed and an elf's toe?'

'Are you really an elf?' asked Jordan.

'No!' he snapped. 'I'm a green pickle! What do you think?'

Jordan smiled. 'I'm Jordan. Do you have a name?'

'Halifax Tickle,' said the elf, still rubbing his toe.

'That's a nice name,' Jordan said. 'Halifax Tickle is like a green pickle.'

But Jordan's smile vanished when she saw something slithering along a corn stalk.

'A horrible snail!' she cried. 'It's eating our plants.'

'Who are you calling horrible?' snapped Halifax Tickle. 'That snail is Slimy.'

'I know it's slimy!' Jordan picked up the snail by its shell.

'I'll give it to the birds.'

'Don't you dare!' screamed the elf. 'Slimy is his name! He's my pet!' He snatched the snail from Jordan. 'Look! You've scared him! He's gone into his shell.'

Jordan was going to say sorry but, at that moment, a jet of water hit them both. The elf fell backwards, the snail in his hand.

Mike was watering the corn with the garden hose.

The elf was wet and now so angry he could hardly squeak. 'Go away, you nasties! Get out of my garden!'

'I beg your pardon, but this is our garden,' said Mike, trying to be polite.

'No it isn't!' the elf screamed. 'It's mine! Mine, mine, mine! Do you hear?'

Jordan and Mike tried to explain, but elves have terrible tempers and Halifax Tickle would not listen, so they went to their teacher.

Mrs Poutu smiled at them and said, 'Elves live in fairytale books. They do not live in gardens.'

'This one lives in our garden,' said Jordan.

'He's green,' said Mike.

'He's got big flat feet and a pet snail called Slimy.'

'That's a good story, Mike,' said Mrs Poutu. 'You should write that down for the story competition.'

'But it's a true story, Mrs Poutu,' said Jordan. 'The elf is real!'

'We'll all go to the garden,' said Mrs Poutu. 'I think you'll find that your elf is just a funny-shaped green plant.'

Twenty children and one big person were too much for Halifax Tickle. When he saw them advancing across the school lawn, he picked up Slimy and rushed off, grumbling. Another good home had been lost.

Jordan saw him running through the curly peas. 'Look!' she cried.

Mrs Poutu blinked. 'Where?'

'Over there!' cried Jordan.

Mrs Poutu laughed. 'That's just a pickle plant!' she said. Then she bent down to look at the ground. She saw prints made by flat feet with long big toes. Beside them, lay a tiny willow-wood hoe, no bigger than a toothbrush.

'Well, I never!' said Mrs Poutu.

As for Halifax Tickle, he was in such a bad mood that he did not go back for his hoe. He ran down the road, puffing and muttering to himself. This time he would look for a big garden full of trees and wild weeds, where he and Slimy could live in peace.

Marvellous Treasure

 Year after year, Captain Polly Molly Macaroon hunted for treasure with her friends. They sailed their ships over shimmery seas.

They dived to search the shadowy wrecks that lay on the ocean floor. They talked about treasure. At untidy pirate parties, they sang about treasure. But the truth was, they never found any.

One day, when Captain Polly Molly Macaroon was by herself on an island, she tripped over something in the long dry grass. It was the edge of a brass box, and inside that box was marvellous treasure. Polly Molly could not believe her eyes. Silver and gold! Diamond and pearls! Money and mounds of glittering jewels!

She heard her friends calling on the other side of the island. 'Yoo-hoo! Polly Molly! Where are you?'

'They'll find my treasure!' she said to herself, and she hid in the long grass with the brass box. She waited for more than an hour, until her friends had gone back to their boat.

'I must put this treasure in a safe place before someone steals it,' she said. 'I know. I'll make a strong wooden cupboard to hide it in.'

With tools from her ship, she sawed and hammered, and hammered and sawed, and made a strong cupboard with a padlock on the door. She was very pleased with her work, but after a while she said to herself, 'Someone could break open the lock on this cupboard. Then where would I be? The cupboard needs a robber-proof room.'

So she hammered and sawed and sawed and hammered and made a robber-proof room with a heavy door and no windows.

But still, Captain Polly Molly Macaroon was not satisfied. 'A room is no good without a house. I will build a pirate house around this room and my treasure will be safe.'

She drew a plan for a house like a fortress. Then she sawed and sawed and sawed, and hammered and hammered and hammered. After many weeks, the pirate house was finished. It had bars on all the windows and seven locks on each door.

But Polly Molly could not rest. 'The house by itself is not enough. It needs high walls around it.'

So, with a lot more hammering and sawing, she made high wooden walls that shut out her view of the sea.

'Now no one can get in,' she said. 'My treasure is safe at last.'

Captain Polly Molly Macaroon should have been happy. The truth was, her heart was as heavy as an anchor. At night she dreamed that she was with her friends sailing the shimmery seas, and she cried salty tears.

Looking for treasure was much more fun than finding it, she decided.

One morning, she heard voices outside the walls of her house. 'Yoo-hoo! Polly Molly! We're going to hunt for treasure. Do you want to come?'

She jumped up. It was not a dream. Her friends were calling on the wild sea wind.

Out of the house she ran, and over the wall she went, her heart as light as a feather. 'Wait for me!' she called.

The marvellous treasure was left behind in the strong cupboard, in the robber-proof room, in the big pirate house with the wall around it.

As far as anyone knows, it is still there.

The Tiny Woman

The tiny woman sat in her shoebox cottage and dreamed of adventure. On Monday she washed her clothes but that was not adventure. On Tuesday she mended her coat with cobweb and a fish–bone needle. On Wednesday she rode her fat, grey mouse to Kitchen Town. She came back with six peanuts and a toothpick umbrella. Thursday was baking day. Roasted peanuts! On Friday, the tiny woman cried, 'I can't live this boring life one more boring day! I'm out of here!'

The fat, grey mouse liked boredom. It didn't want to leave the land of House for the dangerous land of Yard. But the tiny woman was on its back, one hand holding its whiskers, the other waving the toothpick umbrella. 'Giddy-up!' she cried.

Off they went, across the carpet to the gap under the door. A moment later, they were in the wide open spaces of Yard. 'Oh bliss!' cried the tiny woman. 'Adventure! Here we come.'

The mouse crept over to a small jungle, its legs trembling with fear. It had heard stories of a hungry Yard cat and it wanted to run back to the safety of House. But the tiny woman had one hand clenched on its shivering whiskers. She waved the umbrella. 'Hurry!' she cried. 'Gallopy! Gallopy!'

The mouse did not gallop. It tiptoed past a snail and a couple of earwigs, then it stopped as still as a fat, grey stone. Dead ahead, two yellow lamps glowed in a red petunia bush. Sure enough, it was the Yard cat!

The yellow eyes stared and the ragged ears twitched. The mouth was a grin full of pointy teeth.

'What an amazing creature!' cried the tiny woman. 'It's so big, so – oh dear!'

The Yard cat had swiped at them with a paw full of claws.

Hiss-ss-ss!

The mouse squeaked in terror and ran inside a hose pipe, scraping the tiny woman off its back. She sat on the ground, her hair in a mess. 'Go away,' she cried, poking at the cat with her toothpick umbrella.

The cat thought she was a new kind of bee with a very big sting. The cat had once eaten a bee. It would not do that again. It hissed through its pointy teeth and walked away through the jungle.

The tiny woman banged her umbrella against the drain pipe. 'You can come out now,' she called to the fat, grey mouse.

As she climbed on the mouse's back, the tiny woman cried, 'On we go to more adventure! Gallopy! Gallopy!'

But the mouse did not want more adventure. It shivered all over and turned for home. With the woman tugging at its whiskers, it ran as fast as it could back to the boring land of House.

At that moment, the Yard cat decided that the umbrella was not a bee's sting, after all. But it was too late. While the cat hissed and hunted in the petunias, the tiny woman and the mouse sat in their shoebox cottage, eating roasted peanuts.

The Grumpysaurus

 Jojo and Brett wanted a singing lizard from the Rare Pets Shop but Mum bought a plain old grumpysaurus. As soon as she came in the gate, Jojo heard the moaning.

'What a dump! What a terrible dump! You expect me to live in a place like this?'

'Oh, no!' Jojo called to her mother. 'Not a grumpysaurus! My teacher's got a grumpysaurus and she can't give it away!'

The grumpysaurus rolled its eyes and gave a sigh that

withered the pot plant in the back porch. 'Nobody likes me! Everybody hates me!'

Mum, who was very kind, said, 'Don't say that! We like you.'

But it was too late. The grumpysaurus waddled as far as the kitchen and had a tantrum. It lay on its back by the fridge, and kicked its scaly feet. 'People are horrible to poor little me! I wish I'd never been hatched.'

Mum tried hard. She said, 'Stop! We more than like you. We love you! Honest!'

But just then, Brett came in. 'I don't believe it!' he cried. 'You got us a grumpysaurus!' and he put his fingers in his ears.

By the time Dad came home, the grumpysaurus was howling on the living room floor. Dad looked at the wet carpet. 'Are you sure these are tears?' he asked.

'It's having a few settling-in problems, but it'll be better tomorrow,' said Mum.

'No, it won't,' said Brett. 'A grumpysaurus is grumpy because that's the way they are. It has to go back to the shop.'

'We can't take it back,' Mum said. 'I got it at sale price – no returns.'

At that, the grumpysaurus yelled louder. 'Nobody likes me! People are horrible. People are unkind. My life is a miserable pain in the never-you-mind.'

Mum put a full plate of meat pie and vegetables on the carpet beside it. 'Have some dinner,' she said. 'A full stomach will make you feel better.'

The grumpysaurus ate the dinner in one big gulp. Then it yelled, 'That was the worst food I've ever tasted! Help! Police! You're trying to poison me!'

Nothing pleased the grumpysaurus. It moaned and groaned all day, and it wasn't long before the family caught the grumps. Dad argued with Mum. Mum argued with Jojo, and Jojo fought with Brett. Brett kicked a hole in his bedroom door.

'This must stop!' said Dad. 'Misery is as infectious as measles. The grumpysaurus must go before our family is ruined by grumpiness!'

'That's right! Blame me!' bellowed the grumpysaurus and it had another tantrum.

Brett shook his head. 'No one will take it from us.'

'I'm sorry,' said Mum. 'I shouldn't have bought it. But it looked so lonely, I thought we could offer it friendship and a little happiness.'

Dad said, 'My dear, a grumpysaurus is happy when it's miserable. The more it yells and sobs, the happier it gets. But I can't stand it one more day.'

Jojo looked at the grumpysaurus which was kicking the couch and biting the cushions. 'My teacher says that the only friend for a grumpysaurus is another grumpysaurus.'

'No!' said Dad. 'Definitely not!'

Brett looked at his family and grinned. 'Hey!' he said. 'I've got an idea!'

That afternoon, Mum and Dad bought an extra garden shed, big enough for two grumpysauruses. When it was in place at the far end of the back yard, Jojo offered to take her teacher's grumpysaurus.

'It was my brother's idea,' Jojo explained to her teacher. 'He says our grumpysaurus will live happily ever after with another grumpysaurus and it will leave us alone.'

Brett was right. Their grumpysaurus and the teacher's grumpysaurus moved into the shed in the back garden. With twice the moaning and groaning, they were very happy. The family was equally happy to have a house free of grumpiness.

'Ah, the peace!' said Dad, stretching out with his hands behind his head. 'It's utter bliss!'

Mum hugged him. 'Now the misery disease has gone, I think we're more appreciative of each other than we were before I bought the grumpysaurus.'

'Oh, I wouldn't say that,' Dad replied, but the others could tell from his smile that he thought it.

'Are two grumpysauruses called grumpysauri?' Brett wanted to know.

'Probably,' said Jojo. 'But what does it matter – as long as we can't hear their moaning.'

It was true that the house remained peaceful, and when there was a double grumpysaurus tantrum in the far-off garden shed, the family just closed their windows.

The Bag of Smiles

 Once there was a king who was very unhappy. He was so miserable that he hated to see other people enjoying themselves. He made a law that in his kingdom no one was allowed to laugh or smile. 'If you do,' he said, 'you will be severely punished.'

This meant that people could not tell jokes. Neither could they have parties for fear of accidentally smiling. So everyone walked around looking as though they were eating lemons.

Did I say everyone? Not quite! On the edge of that kingdom there were a man, a woman, a cat, a dog and five chickens who were happy all the time. They didn't know about the law that said, No smiling or laughing. They laughed all day, and even smiled in their sleep at night.

The grumpy king heard about them, and he was very angry. He called his guards and went out to the farm where the man, the woman, the cat, the dog and the five chickens were happily at work.

'How dare you laugh and smile!' the king roared. 'Don't you know it's against the law?'

'But we've always laughed and smiled,' said the woman.

'We didn't know we weren't supposed to do that,' said the man.

'That's no excuse!' snarled the king. 'You will be punished! I am going to take your smiles away!'

The king had his guards bring over a round leather bag. First, he took the man's smile and put it in the bag. Then he snatched the woman's smile and the dog's happy grin. Into the bag they went. After that he took the cat's smile and the smiles of the five chickens so that the bag was almost full. He tied a cord around the top and added a big heavy stone.

'Guards!' he bellowed. 'Take this bag of smiles and drop it in the deepest part of the sea!' Then he turned to the man and woman, the cat and dog, and the five chickens. 'You will never smile again!' he snarled.

Now, any king as miserable as that does not last long. Within a year, he died of a bad case of grumpiness and a new king ruled the kingdom. The new king was a happy man. At once, he changed the law so that everyone could laugh and smile. What a difference that made! People told jokes. They had parties and picnics, and the streets rang with laughter.

Out on the farm, however, there wasn't a hint of humour. 'I don't think we'll ever laugh again,' sighed the woman. 'Our smiles are lost forever.'

The man nodded glumly. 'Let us ask the new king if he can help us find them.'

The happy new king was very sympathetic. 'The deepest part of the sea?' he said. 'That is difficult, but not impossible. I know a clever dolphin who may be able to help.'

He took the man, the woman, the cat, the dog and the five chickens to the seaside in his royal limousine. There, at the end of a jetty, he put his fingers in his mouth and

whistled for his dolphin friend. When she answered
his call, he told her about the leather bag of smiles. She
nodded, as dolphins do, and away she went, swimming
down the sloping sea bed: past the crabs and starfish,
down past shoals of silver herring, down to the depths
where the wrecks of ships lay. Still further she went,
down into the deepest part of the sea where only the

sea monsters dared swim. There she found the bag of smiles, lying in the mud.

The dolphin grabbed the bag in her mouth and swam for the surface. But the cord on the bag had rotted. The stone fell away, and some of the smiles came out and stuck on the dolphin's face.

Well, as you may guess, the man and the woman were very pleased to get their smiles back. So were the cat and the dog. But where were the smiles for the chickens?

Today, cats smile. Dogs frequently laugh. Chickens, on the other hand, never smile. If you want to know why, look at a dolphin. It has a smile so big, it looks like five smiles in one.

The Travelling Bath

 Mr West liked nothing better than to loll in a hot bath with a morning cup of coffee in one hand, and the newspaper in the other. He sometimes got soap in his cup and a wet crossword, but these were small problems.

The big problem was that a long loll in the bath made him late for his work at the hardware store.

Mr West's boss detested lateness. It made him grumpy all day.

'I'm sorry,' said Mr West, running his fingers through

his wet hair. 'I forgot the time again.'

'Harrumph,' said his boss. 'You can stay in tonight after the shop has closed. Perhaps sweeping the floor will teach you a lesson.'

This meant that Mr West was late for his meal of a cold lamb chop and cold mashed potato.

'My dear,' said his wife. 'You love your morning bath. Why don't you fit the bath with wheels and a motor, then you can travel to work in it. You will never be late again.'

Mr West's eyes shone. 'What a wonderful idea! My angel, you are so clever!'

Being clever himself, it didn't take him long to fit the bath with wheels, a steering lever, and a little engine that moved the bath and heated the water. His problem was solved. He could have a long loll in a scented bubble bath while travelling down the street. True, people did stare at him but they soon got used to the bath chugging along the pavement with Mr West sipping his coffee and reading the latest news about the government.

For the first few weeks, Mr West carried his work clothes and a towel in a waterproof case that fitted under the tub. He got changed in the back room where the bath was emptied down the drain and then, at lunchtime, Mr West would take it back to his house so that Mrs West could have her bath.

But as summer faded and mornings grew cold, Mr West was more reluctant to get out of that bath. He found that he could easily steer it around the hardware shop, serving customers. Once he dropped an electric drill into the bubbles but mostly he was very careful. The sight of a salesman in a bath attracted lots of customers, so the boss didn't mind.

The person who did mind was Mrs West. She was a nurse with an afternoon shift at the hospital, and she could not have a bath before she went to work. Having a cold shower outside with the hose was not the same as soaking in nice hot bubbles.

Fed up, she stormed down to the hardware shop where Mr West was sitting in his tub, showing a crowd of customers how the new gas barbecues worked.

'I need the tub!' she said.

'Not now, dear,' replied Mr West. 'Can't you see I'm busy?'

'Yes! Now!' cried Mrs West, and with one swoop of her hand, she pulled out the plug on its chain.

Water and foam poured over the floor of the hardware shop. Mr West tried to snatch back the plug but Mrs West waved it over her head like a lasso.

Soon the bath was completely empty which was very embarrassing for Mr West. He couldn't reach his towel and had to cover himself with a sheet of sandpaper.

Meanwhile, the boss came out of his office to see what the fuss was about. He wasn't very pleased.

Mr and Mrs West each tried to tell their side of the story.

'Stop!' the boss yelled, putting his fingers in his ears. 'You need two travelling baths – a His tub and a Her tub. Now, clean up this mess, both of you!'

So now the Wests have two tubs.

Mrs West's bathtub has a pattern of roses on it, but is otherwise like Mr West's. At the moment, she parks it in the ambulance bay at the hospital, but as the days get colder, she will probably steer it around the wards, dishing out tablets that taste like bubble bath.

Zamforan the Dragon

 Zamforan the dragon had a home in a deep, dark cave. But Zamforan the dragon was not keen on deep, dark caves which are usually damp and full of shadows. He wanted a home in a library that had big windows and books about dragons like himself. So he spread his leathery wings and flew, flip-flap, into the town. He landed in the street, folded his wings and waddled through the library doors, happily puffing smoke rings. At the sight of a dragon, people forgot that they wanted to change their books.

They fell over each other as they rushed for the doors and, when they were safely outside, they yelled, 'Go away, Dragon! Get out of our library!'

Zamforan yawned a great puff of smoke and said in a deep gravelly voice, 'Don't tell me to go away. Here I am and here I stay.'

The people of that town definitely did not want a dragon in their library.

'He looks dangerous,' said a woman.

'He's got fire in his nose,' said a man. 'If he sneezes, he'll barbecue our books.'

The mayor of the town went to the library door and peeked in. He said with a nice smile, 'Yoo hoo! Dragon? I will give you a bag of gold if you go back to your deep, dark cave in the mountains.'

Zamforan snorted more smoke. 'I can't read gold. So please don't tell me to go away. Here I am and here I stay.'

The mayor stopped smiling. 'I will call the police!' he said.

Four police officers came running, their silver badges shining in the sun.

'Dragon!' their chief yelled. 'Put your paws up and come out of the library at once!'

The dragon huffed a huge cloud of grey smoke that made everyone cough.

The officer put his handkerchief over his nose and yelled again, 'Come out or we will arrest you!'

Zamforan lay on the carpet and closed his eyes. Tiny points of flame trembled in his nostrils. 'Don't tell me to go away. Here I am and here I stay.'

The police officers were silent. No one wanted to arrest a dragon with a nose that could spout fire.

The police chief called the fire brigade. 'Put out that dragon's fire!' he ordered.

The fire officers dragged their hoses to the library.

'Stop! Stop!' cried the people. 'If you turn on the hoses, you'll wet the books.'

A fire officer said, 'If we don't turn on the hoses, the books could burn.'

The people looked at each other and a discussion began. What sort of books did they want in their library? Soggy books? Or books crisped to cinders?

No one knew what to do.

But not everyone in the town was scared of dragons. A boy called Chu and a girl called Melissa did not mind having a dragon in the library. They walked in to the children's section where Zamforan was reading the sad story of St George and the dragon. Fat, dragonish tears rolled from his eyes and over a sob, he said, 'St George cut off the dragon's head!'

'Hush,' said Melissa. 'You shouldn't read books that upset you.'

'It's only a story,' Chu said quickly.

Melissa patted the dragon's scaly back. 'Why do you want to live in a library?'

'I was lonely in the deep, dark cave,' Zamforan said. 'In this library there are books about dragons.'

'But they don't all have happy endings,' Chu told him.

'So I see,' said the dragon with a smoky sigh.

Chu looked at Melissa. Melissa looked at Chu. Then Chu said to Zamforan, 'In our friendly school, we have nice books about dragons.'

Melissa nodded and said, 'In our friendly school, we also have very nice teachers. No one will ever turn a hose on you. Promise!'

Since that day, Zamforan the dragon has lived at the very friendly school.

The children read him dragon stories with happy endings and the very nice teachers toast their lunchtime bread on his nose.

Zamforan the dragon smiles and says in his gravelly voice, 'I will never go away. Here I am and here I stay.'

If you ever go past that school, you might like to call in for some dragon toast with melted butter.

My Tiger

 My tiger had a bad tooth. I went with him to the dental nurse.

'Please, nurse,' I said, 'will you fix my tiger's tooth?'

'Is he dangerous?' said the nurse.

'No,' I said. 'He only eats cake.'

'Tell him to sit in the chair,' she said.

My tiger sat in the chair.

He didn't like the drill.

When it hurt him, he cried.

'There,' said the nurse. 'All done. Tell him he's not to have cake again.'

'But he always eats cake,' I said.

'It's bad for him,' she said. 'No more from now on. Do you hear?'

'Then what can he eat?' I said.

'The same as other tigers,' she said.

So my tiger ate the dental nurse.

Other Gecko Press books by Joy Cowley and Gavin Bishop
Snake and Lizard (2007)
Friends: Snake and Lizard (2009)

Other Gecko Press books by Joy Cowley
(illustrated by Sarah Davis)
The Fierce Little Woman and the Wicked Pirate (2010)

Other Gecko Press books by Gavin Bishop
There was a Crooked Man (2009)
There was an Old Woman (2008)